birdnoclue.com
also on AMAZON

© 2018 K. MOOSE COOPER
First Edition

ISBN 978-1-7327680-1-7

The Bird Who Had No Clue

(it was a bird)

by K. Moose Cooper

for

Dan (dD & Kz)
and Wayne

The bird
    woke up late

The bird broke
    through its shell

            and said...

"Who am I?

Where am I?

Where is
everyone
else?"

The bird
saw no
helper

The bird
saw no
help

and said ...

"I guess I will
have to learn
things for
myself"

So with nobody there
to help the bird out,

the bird
looked
above

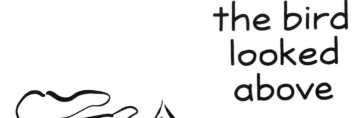

and the bird
looked about...

for someone to follow

to figure things out...

The bird
tried to be
like a bee
for an hour...

but no matter
<u>how</u> hard
it tried...

it kept
crushing
the flowers

The bird
 tried to live
 in a hole
  like a mole...

but found it
  too dirty
   too damp
    and too cold

The bird
even tried

to swim like
a fish

but found water too wet...

The bird didn't know
what else to try

where else to go

or how, when,
or why

The bird felt so _sad_

that it started to cry

But then above
in the dark ...

the bird
  saw a light...

The bird saw the moon

glowing happy and bright,

and said...

"I wish I could shine like the moon in the night..."

And then when morning came...

the bird saw a balloon

and said ...

"I wish <u>I</u> could fly the same way someday, too"

Then the bird
 saw a beautiful
   butterfly
    flutter...

and said...

"I wish I
 had wings
   with beautiful
     colors..."

singing songs without a care

and stood

and stared...

and said... "What is <u>that</u> having fun up <u>there</u>?!"

"What do you mean?"
said an ant,

who was
enjoying a sit,

"That *bird* is like you,
And you are like it!"

"No, I am <u>not</u>"

said the bird
to the ant

"That `bird`
as you call it
does things
that I <u>can't</u>!"

"My friend...
 you don't <u>know</u>?

And yet you've made it
 so far!

Well, I think I can help you
 right where we are

Do me
 a favor..."

"...because the thing that you are...

is a <u>bird</u>

and no other!"

"Wait.

You mean <u>I'm</u> a *bird*?"

said the bird
to the ant

but of course!

"You mean
 I can do...

 all the things...

 that I <u>can't</u>?"

The bird flew
 off the ground!

sing-songy
  bird sounds?..."

"You mean
  I can shine...

... like the shiniest things?"

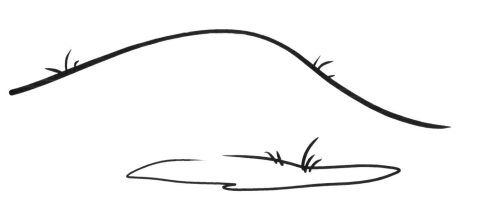

And in the light
of the sun,

the bird was
quite stunned...

to see ...

≥ colors ≥

right under its wings!

The bird was free now <u>because</u>
it had learned what <u>it was</u>...

It could **shine**
its bright colors

It could **fly**
and be flappy

goodbye
my friend!

I will
miss
you!

...and **sing** bird-songs all day

'cause it finally was <u>happy</u>!

But though it saw
 many new places,
  the bird always
    returned...

to the ant
 the bird loved,

Yay!

who loved
the bird
in return

And they'd take off <u>together</u>

in the sun

flying free...

two good friends having fun, with a whole world to see...

now that the bird
was the bird ...

it had learned
it could be!

And then one day
  in the woods

    fell an egg, all alone...

    It bounced
      from a branch

      and stopped
       near a stone...

And out popped
a beak ...

and two
curious eyes,

staring above ...

... at a bird in the sky

Made in the USA
Middletown, DE
21 November 2018